Franke
Doesn't Plant
Petunias

There are more books about the Bailey School Kids!
Have you read these adventures?

Vampires Don't Wear Polka Dots
Santa Claus Doesn't Mop Floors
Leprechauns Don't Play Basketball
Werewolves Don't Go to Summer Camp
Ghosts Don't Eat Potato Chips

Frankenstein Doesn't Plant Petunias

by Debbie Dadey
and
Marcia Thornton Jones

illustrated by John Steven Gurney

A
LITTLE **APPLE**
PAPERBACK

SCHOLASTIC INC.

New York Toronto London Auckland Sydney

To Thelma Kuhljuergen Thornton —
everyone should have a mom
as great as you! — MTJ

To Lillie Mae Bailey —
the best grandmother ever! — DD

ISBN 0-590-47071-X

14 13 12 11 10 9 8 7 6 5 4 3 3 4 5 6 7 8/9

Printed in the U.S.A. 40

First Scholastic printing, May 1993

Contents

1
Field Trip

Melody twisted her black pigtail and looked out the bus window at the cloudy sky. "I can't wait to get to the Shelley Museum."

Mrs. Jeepers' third-grade class from Bailey Elementary School was on a bus heading for the Shelley Museum of Science. It was the last field trip before summer vacation. Melody was sitting in the middle of the bus with her friends Liza, Eddie, and Howie.

Howie nodded. "This is the best field trip ever!"

Eddie made a face. "Other kids get to go to Water World, but we have to go to an old science museum."

"Science museums can be a lot of fun," Melody told her friends. "I went to one in Indianapolis that was incredible."

"It's incredible that they didn't keep you for an exhibit." Eddie giggled.

"If the Shelley Museum is doing experiments on smart alecks, you'd better watch out." Melody stuck out her tongue at Eddie.

The kids on the bus bounced up and

down as they went over an old bridge. "My mother told me that the museum was closed after an electrical storm damaged the building," Melody said. "This is the first time it's been open in fourteen years. It's supposed to have lots of new stuff, even a prehistoric exhibit."

"Maybe there's a bat exhibit and Mrs. Jeepers can visit her friends," Eddie joked.

"Shhh, she's looking this way," Melody whispered. The four kids smiled as Mrs. Jeepers looked back from the front seat. Her long fire-red hair was neatly pulled back by a green bow. Purple fingernails gently rubbed the emerald-green brooch on her polka-dotted dress.

When Mrs. Jeepers turned to speak to the bus driver, Eddie bragged, "I'm not afraid of Mrs. Jeepers. I don't care if she is Count Dracula's cousin."

Mrs. Jeepers was from Transylvania and seemed to have special powers, especially when she rubbed her brooch. Most of the kids in the third grade at Bailey Elementary thought she was a vampire.

"I hope we get there soon," Liza said in a small voice. "This bus is making me sick."

"Hold on!" Howie said. "I think I see the museum."

"All I see is dust." Eddie coughed as they turned onto a dirt road. Dust filled the bus as it bounced from one pothole to another.

The kids covered their noses until the bus lurched to a stop. When the dust settled, they looked out the grimy windows.

"Now I *know* Mrs. Jeepers is batty," Eddie said.

2
The Shelley Museum

Everyone filed off the bus and stared up at the old museum. It was four stories tall and stood on the top of a hill surrounded by towering oak trees. Shingles were missing from the roof, and broken shutters banged in the wind. The whole building needed a paint job.

"This place looks like it's ready to fall in a heap," Melody said.

"I guess they never got around to fixing it after it was struck by lightning," Howie said.

"Maybe lightning fried the owner's brains." Eddie laughed.

A distant rumble of thunder could be heard as dark clouds swirled above.

"All right, children." Mrs. Jeepers clapped her hands. "Let us begin our tour." As she led the class up the crumbling steps of the museum, the yellow school bus disappeared down the long dirt road.

"Do you still feel sick?" Melody asked Liza. "You look a little pale."

Liza pulled her jacket tight and shrugged. "There's something very strange about this place."

"Like what?" Howie asked.

"I've seen it before," she said.

"But you've never been here," Melody said.

"I haven't," Liza whispered. "That's why it bothers me."

"Boogers bother you." Eddie rolled his eyes. "Come on, we have to catch up."

Mrs. Jeepers and the rest of the class were gathered in front of a huge wooden door.

"Where's the doorbell?" Carey asked.

Mrs. Jeepers smiled an odd little half smile. "This is a very old building. We must use the door knocker." She lifted the heavy iron knocker and let it fall with a thud.

There was no answer.

The third-graders huddled by the door. "Maybe no one's home," Liza said.

"Nonsense." Mrs. Jeepers smiled. "They are expecting us."

"I hope they hurry," Carey said. "It's starting to rain, and the bus won't be back for hours."

Then the door slowly creaked open.

3

Dr. Victor and Frank

Lightning cracked across the sky as Mrs. Jeepers and the third-graders stared up at a towering giant of a man. His long legs stuck out of his brown ragged pants, and a wrinkled white shirt stretched across his massive chest. His square face was pale next to his coal-black hair, and across his cheek was a huge purple scar.

"He's got a gun," Howie whispered to his friends. He pointed to the man's pocket where the handle of a pistol peeped out. The third-graders took one step away from the hulk as he glared down at the group of kids.

Mrs. Jeepers stretched out her hand and smiled. "Hello, I am Mrs. Jeepers,

and this is my class from Bailey Elementary School. We are here to visit the museum."

The giant lifted one enormous hand and pushed the door back. An ugly scar reached all around his bony wrist.

"Hrrmm," he grunted as Mrs. Jeepers walked in. The third-graders followed, staying as far from the giant as possible.

"Did you see that waffle face?" Eddie whispered when they were inside the entrance hall.

Howie nodded. "He has more scars than I have freckles."

"He's so tall," Melody whispered. "I've never seen anyone that big before."

The big man led them down a dark hall. Science exhibits filled the rooms on both sides. Tables covered with rocks lined the hall, and huge posters of labeled rocks covered the cracked walls.

"I could have stayed in my driveway and had more fun playing with the gravel," Eddie fussed.

"Quit complaining, Eddie," Melody snapped. "You know you'd rather be here than at school doing math."

"Math is starting to look better and better," Eddie whispered as they were led into a room full of mummies.

A small man in a white jacket greeted them. "That will be all, Frank. You have work to do elsewhere in the museum."

"Hrrmm." Frank glared down at the children once more before disappearing down a dark hallway.

The small man greeted the students, his eyes darting from face to face. "Welcome to the Shelley Museum. I am

the museum curator, Dr. Victor. And I see you've already met my assistant, Frank. I am looking forward to showing you the museum. I think you will be amazed."

"I think it's already amazing," Eddie whispered.

"What do you mean?" asked Howie.

"It's incredible that a weasel and a giant run a museum!"

"It's more incredible than you think," Liza muttered to her friends as the rest of the class followed Dr. Victor into the next room. "I have to tell you something."

"What's your problem?" Eddie asked.

"You have been acting strange," Melody said. "What's wrong?"

"You'll just laugh," Liza said.

"No, we won't." Melody gave Eddie a dirty look. "Will we, Eddie?"

Eddie rolled his eyes. "Nothing she says surprises me."

The three kids huddled around Liza. "My older brother had to read a book for an English report," Liza said softly. "He read it to me to scare me."

"Book reports scare me, too," Eddie snickered.

Liza shook her head. "I wasn't scared. At least not then, because it didn't seem real. But now it does."

"What was the book about?" Howie asked.

Liza took a shaky breath and began. "Long ago, a young scientist started secret experiments. He sneaked into cemeteries late at night to steal what he needed. Then he worked hundreds of hours putting his creation together."

Liza paused. Outside, the wind hissed, and a tree limb scraped against a window. The kids jumped, and then looked back at Liza.

"What was the creation?" Howie whispered.

"It was a monster brought back from the dead."

"That's disgusting," Melody said.

Eddie slapped Liza on the back. "I think it's cool."

"But it wasn't," Liza told him. "The scientist was afraid of his own creation. He fled, and the monster was forced to fend for himself."

"A monster ought to be able to take care of himself," Eddie said. "I do it all the time."

Liza shook her head. "It's easy for you. You're only half as hideous as the monster."

"That's a matter of opinion," Melody joked.

"What happened to the monster?" Howie interrupted.

"For a while, he roamed through the woods. He loved nature, especially flowers. But when people saw him they were so frightened, they tried to kill him. He was deathly afraid of fire, and people chased him with torches. The monster had no choice. He had to kill — or be killed."

"That's terrible," Melody said.

"What's the name of that story, anyway?" Howie asked.

Liza looked at her friends before answering. *"Frankenstein."*

"I saw that movie on the late show," Eddie said. "What does that have to do with this old museum?"

Liza spoke softly. "This museum looks just like a picture in the book."

"Then where's the monster?" Howie asked as thunder rumbled overhead.

Liza's face grew pale. "We just saw the monster. And his name is Frank."

4
Bubbles

"Your brain has more bubbles than this room," Eddie told Liza when they caught up with the rest of the class. The third-graders were at the Science Fun exhibit, making bubbles. Bubbles of all sizes filled the air.

"Liza, you're jumping to conclusions," Howie said. "This place is neat." He grabbed a wand and made a

bubble the size of a basketball.

"There aren't any monsters here." Melody giggled as she picked up a wand. "Look at my square bubble!"

"Check out the Bubble Head," Eddie said as he covered Liza with a huge bubble. Liza popped it and gave Eddie a shove. He landed with his hands in a big tub of soapy water.

Melody jumped out of Eddie's way. "All this water reminds me that I have to find a bathroom. Come with me, Liza."

Liza looked down the dark hall. "I don't want to go. Besides, I'm making a star bubble."

"If you don't come right now, you'll be seeing stars," Melody insisted.

Thunder boomed as the girls headed down a dark hall. They peeked into several rooms full of display cases. Finally, Melody found a bathroom.

"Now, can we go back?" Liza asked.

Melody nodded. "I think it's this way."

"I thought it was that way!" Liza said, pointing the other way.

"No, we go *this* way," Melody said, "I'm sure."

"You're all mixed up," Liza said. "I

could swear the bubble room is back there."

Just then a crash came from where Liza was pointing.

"You're right," said Melody. "That must be Eddie."

The two girls made their way down the hall and pushed open a heavy door. What they saw made them gulp.

5
Planting Petunias

Spotlights lit up a small greenhouse connected to the museum. Red and purple petunias filled the greenhouse. Sweet-smelling roses and huge purple orchids were mixed in with the petunias making a sea of brilliant blossoms.

Frank towered over the colorful plants. Very gently, he pushed the lush green leaves aside to spray the soil with water from a water gun.

"There's Howie's gun." Melody giggled. "Frank must really like flowers."

"Frankenstein's monster loved flowers, too," Liza whispered.

"Shhh," Melody warned. "He heard you!"

"Hrrmm," Frank growled and faced

the girls. Then he lunged at them with the gun still in his hand.

"Let's get out of here before he catches us!" Liza squealed and fled down the hall.

"Hrrmm," Frank grunted and came after them. The floor shook with each step he took.

"We're going to die just because *you* had to go to the bathroom," Liza said as they raced away.

"Shut up and run faster," Melody yelled as they rounded a corner.

Plop! They ran smack into Howie and Eddie. "Aren't you girls a little late for the Indianapolis 500?" Eddie asked.

"Where have you been?" Howie asked.

"Never mind that," Melody shrieked. "Frank's after us. Run for your lives!"

"Here he comes!" Liza yelled.

"Hrrmm. *Hrrmm!*" The four kids

raced away from the giant until they came to a dead-end hall.

"Now what do we do?" Liza cried.

"We play pick a door." Eddie pointed to the three closed doors in the hallway. "Do you choose door number one, number two, or number three?"

"Door number three," Melody said, and the four scooted into the room just as they heard Frank coming down the hall. Liza bit her lip, and Melody crossed her fingers. Nobody breathed until Frank's groans faded away.

"Whew. That was too close." Liza sighed.

"Why was old hot dog breath chasing you, anyway?" Eddie asked.

"I don't know," Liza admitted. "But did you happen to notice where we are?"

The four kids stared at the brightly lit room. It was dark outside the window, but inside the room sparkled. Bright white cabinets brimming with crystal-clean glass beakers lined the walls. Strange equipment sat on the counters, and a long table was near a window. A funny odor filled the room.

"It looks like my dad's laboratory," Howie told them.

"I have a weird feeling about this," Liza whispered as lightning streaked across the sky.

6
Eyeball Stew

"You'd have a weird feeling about Beenie Weenies." Eddie laughed.

Howie picked up a beaker full of foaming ooze. "Liza may have a point. Look at this."

Eddie reached for the beaker. "Great. I was a little thirsty."

"Don't drink that," Liza squealed.

"I was just joking," Eddie snapped.

"Quit kidding around and come over here," Melody interrupted. She pointed to an enormous silver door.

Eddie shrugged. "Big deal. It's just a walk-in refrigerator. They have those at the Burger Doodle restaurant."

"Why would anyone need such a big

refrigerator in a laboratory?" Howie wondered out loud.

"Why would Dr. Victor need a laboratory in the first place? After all, this is a museum," Melody said. "And why would he keep his refrigerator locked?"

"Maybe he's working on creating another Frankenstein monster," Liza murmured as lightning flashed outside.

"Liza, if you had a brain you'd be dangerous." Eddie slapped the large silver refrigerator door.

"Maybe that's what's in this refrigerator," Melody told them.

"What?" Howie asked.

"Brains. And other body parts," Melody said.

"I've heard of brain sandwiches before, but that's disgusting," Howie said.

"How about finger sandwiches and eyeball stew," Eddie giggled.

"I bet you're right," Liza nodded.

Eddie pretended to throw up. "You

think Dr. Victor eats eyeball stew?"

"No, spaghetti brains," Liza snapped. "I think Dr. Victor is really Dr. Victor Frankenstein and he uses body parts to make monsters."

Eddie laughed. "I wish you'd get this Frankenstein business out of *your* brain."

No one noticed that the laboratory door had slowly opened behind them as Eddie laughed. Thunder shook the old museum, and then the lights went dead.

7
Hobby

"Aahhh!" Liza screamed and grabbed Eddie's arm. "What happened?"

Eddie knocked Liza's arm away. "The storm caused the lights to go out. There's no reason to squeeze the life out of me."

"We'll never find our way back in the dark," Melody gulped.

The laboratory was so dark, the four kids couldn't see their hands in front of them.

"Did you hear that?" Liza squealed. "It sounded like knuckles cracking!"

"Maybe it was some leftover fingers in the refrigerator getting some exercise." Eddie laughed.

"There's nothing funny about monsters living near Bailey City." Liza would've kicked Eddie's leg, but she couldn't find one in the dark.

"Speaking of monsters," a voice behind them said, "what are you third-grade monsters doing in my lab?"

"It's Dr. Victor," Melody gulped again.

Dr. Victor switched on a flashlight. The weak beam of light glowed on his face, making his eyes look like dark holes.

"Don't they teach you to read at Bailey Elementary?" Dr. Victor shined the flashlight on the open laboratory door. Big red letters spelled PRIVATE — DO NOT ENTER.

"We didn't see the sign," Melody apologized.

"We're s-s-sorry," Howie stammered. "We g-g-got lost."

Dr. Victor cracked his knuckles. "It is safest to stay with your teacher."

"Why?" Eddie blurted.

Dr. Victor smiled. His teeth were bright in the flashlight beam. "These halls are confusing. You might easily be lost in the museum for hours. It could be most unfortunate."

"Especially with a monster lurking in the shadows," Liza mumbled.

Dr. Victor glared at her before continuing. "Mrs. Jeepers has been very worried. If you will follow me I will take you to her and we will end this unfortunate incident."

"We would appreciate that," Howie said.

"And I would appreciate it if you would put this laboratory out of your mind," Dr. Victor said as he led them down the hall. "It has long been a hobby of mine to tinker in a lab, and I would like to keep it private."

"We understand," Melody told him. "Everybody has hobbies. I like to collect stamps."

"But very few people collect monsters," Liza muttered to herself as she followed Dr. Victor down the long dark hallway.

8
Big Bones

"I am disappointed in your behavior," Mrs. Jeepers told the four kids. Dr. Victor had taken them to the dinosaur exhibit. The rest of the class was sitting on benches beside huge replicas of a tyrannosaurus rex and an apatosaurus. Mrs. Jeepers and some of the kids were holding flashlights.

"I'm sorry," Melody explained. "I had to go to the bathroom."

"And then we got lost," Liza added.

Mrs. Jeepers rubbed her brooch and flashed her green eyes. "Do not let it happen again. As for our field trip, we may have to postpone the rest of the museum until the lights come back on."

"No need for that," Dr. Victor said.

"One charming thing about old buildings is that there are always plenty of candles." He held up a huge flaming candelabra. The light from the candelabra cast eerie shadows behind the life-sized dinosaur statues.

"Please explore to your heart's desire." Dr. Victor smiled.

"All right!" Eddie cheered and grabbed a plastic dinosaur bone the size of a broom. "If I had bones this size, nobody would mess with me."

"That is very true," Dr. Victor told him. "I have always thought that a larger species of humans would make the world a better place." He placed one candelabra next to the bone table. "Now, I must light more candles." Dr. Victor disappeared behind a group of third-graders.

"Did you hear that?" Liza squealed. "He wants all human beings to be bigger . . . just like Frank."

"Maybe he's trying to make an improved race of large people," Howie said.

Eddie laughed. "Frank is no monster. He's a great big museum assistant. Just because he's tall doesn't mean he's Dr. Victor's chemical creation brought back from the dead. If that were true, basketball players would be monsters, too."

"It's not that he's tall," Liza told them. "Haven't you noticed his scars?"

Melody nodded. "And Frank likes flowers. Just like Frankenstein's monster."

"You guys have flipped." Eddie laughed. "I saw the movie, and I'm sure of one thing. Frankenstein doesn't plant petunias." Eddie rolled his eyes. "Frank isn't Frankenstein's monster any more than I am."

"Mrs. DeeDee might not agree with you," Melody giggled. Mrs. DeeDee was a teacher who had quit just three weeks after teaching Eddie.

"Very funny," Eddie smirked. "I know Frank isn't the monster and I can prove it."

"How?" Liza asked.

But Eddie didn't get a chance to answer.

9
I Am Not a Man

"*Hrrmm!*" Frank stood near the door of the dinosaur room, staring at the candelabra. "HRRMM!" he bellowed again and backed up against the skeleton of a stegosaurus. The skeleton clattered to the floor as Frank ran from the room.

"It's the candelabra," Melody whispered. "He's afraid of fire."

Liza nodded. "Just like Frankenstein's monster."

Dr. Victor rushed into the room and set two more candelabras on the table. Then he kicked the stegosaurus bones into a heap. "Please excuse my assistant's behavior. He has not been well."

Mrs. Jeepers smiled her odd little half smile. "That is quite all right."

"Please, continue enjoying the dinosaur exhibit," Dr. Victor said. "I will see about finding more lights."

"It's just like a monster to destroy an entire skeleton," Liza whispered to her friends as Dr. Victor left the room.

"I told you," Eddie snapped. "Frank isn't a monster."

"How can you prove it?" Liza asked Eddie.

"There's got to be a way," Eddie shrugged. "I could ask him. 'Oh, by the way, Frank. Are you a Frankenstein monster?'"

"Right. One grunt would mean yes, and two grunts would mean no." Melody giggled.

"Shhh," Howie hissed. "Did you hear that?"

The four kids listened. Outside the museum, rain continued to pound the windows, and the wind howled around the old building.

"All I hear is the storm," Melody said.

"It's a doozy of a storm," Eddie agreed.

Liza shuddered. "I hope the bus can make it back to pick us up. I'd hate to be stuck here."

Crash!

"Now did you hear it?" Howie asked.

The third-graders stopped their exploring to listen. CRASH! CRASH! CRASH!

"It sounds like the building is falling apart," Howie said.

Liza gulped. "Maybe Frank is going

crazy and destroying the whole museum. Just like this poor skeleton."

"Where is Dr. Victor, anyway?" Melody wondered. "After all. This is *his* museum."

Mrs. Jeepers spoke calmly to the class and pointed down the hall. "The sound is coming from there. Stay here. I will check on the problem."

Mrs. Jeepers slowly walked down the dark hall toward the horrible sounds. Her small flashlight wavered in the shadows.

"We can't let her go alone," Melody told them.

"Why not?" Eddie asked. "If she is a vampire, nothing can hurt her. We, on the other hand, could be killed very easily."

"Eddie, for once in your life, be a man and help." Melody grabbed a candelabra from the table.

"In case you haven't noticed, I'm only

four foot three inches tall and in the third grade. I am not a man."

"I thought you wanted to prove Frank wasn't a monster," Melody said.

"I do," Eddie snapped as more crashes came from down the hall. "But Mrs. Jeepers told us to stay here."

"Since when do you do what Mrs. Jeepers wants?" Melody asked.

Howie threw back his shoulders and said bravely, "I'll go with you."

"Me, too," Liza squeaked a little less bravely.

Eddie snatched a flashlight from one of the other third-graders. "All right, I'll go. But I think you guys need to learn more about self-survival." Eddie led the way down the dark hall. Liza walked behind Melody, holding tightly to her arm.

CRASH! "It's coming from behind that door," Melody said.

"Well, open it," Eddie said.

"All right, scaredy-cat, I will." Melody slowly reached out her hand to turn the doorknob.

CRASH! The four kids jumped away from the door. "Maybe we better let Mrs. Jeepers handle this. After all, she is the teacher," Liza squeaked.

"Don't chicken out now," Melody said. She took a deep breath and quickly opened the door.

"Oh, my gosh," Liza screamed. "It's the end of the world!"

10
Greenhouse

"Get a grip on yourself," Eddie hollered. "It's just a storm." Wind whipped past the four kids as they stared into the greenhouse. One entire section of the wall had been ripped away, and rain was pouring onto the tiled floor. Large plants were scattered all over.

Liza screamed and pointed to the far corner where Mrs. Jeepers lay in a heap. "She's hurt." Before her friends could stop her, Liza rushed into the ruined greenhouse. Hail the size of lemons pelted the glass walls and roof of the room. Liza knelt beside Mrs. Jeepers and gently patted her hand. "Wake up, Mrs. Jeepers," she said.

"We better help before she's pulverized by hail," Melody said.

"I think someone else is going to pulverize both of them." Eddie gulped.

Frank appeared through the back door of the greenhouse. He towered over Liza and Mrs. Jeepers. Then he looked around and groaned. "Hrrmm. Hrrmm."

"He's going to kill Liza and Mrs. Jeepers," Howie screamed above the roar of the rain. "They're trapped like flies in a fly trap!"

"*Hrrmm!*" Frank growled at the kids. He took one step toward them, but a huge gust of wind tore the door off its hinges, taking part of the greenhouse wall with it. Frank cried and covered his face as pots of petunias flew past him.

"*Hrrmm!*" He dropped to the ground and crawled after his plants. Rain tore at his white shirt as the wind ripped a plant from his grasp. He struggled to grab more petunias as they blew past him.

"He's trying to save his plants," Melody said.

"Poor Frank," Liza cried. "He's losing his beautiful flowers."

"Poor Frank, nothing," Eddie said.

Suddenly part of the greenhouse roof started to squeak and crack. Frank looked up as it began to fall on Liza and Mrs. Jeepers.

"It's going to kill them!" Howie screamed.

But before the roof smashed to the floor, Frank lunged.

11
Ruined

Frank threw himself over Liza and Mrs. Jeepers, and they all disappeared under a pile of wooden beams.

"I don't believe it!" Eddie yelled. "Frank tried to save their lives."

"Are they alive?" Melody whispered as they made their way over the shattered roof and crushed plants.

When they found Liza and Mrs. Jeepers, Frank was leaning against the wall.

Liza smiled at the giant as she helped Mrs. Jeepers sit up. "Thank you for saving us. Now we'll help you save your petunias."

Before her friends could stop her, Liza chased a purple petunia.

The rain slowed to a steady drizzle as Liza and her friends helped collect the scattered plants. They had just filled a potting table with large red petunias when Dr. Victor rushed into the greenhouse.

"What have you little monsters done now?" he screamed.

Mrs. Jeepers calmly touched her brooch. "The children are helping Frank clean up the damage from the storm. Third-graders from Bailey Elementary are *not* monsters."

"Pardon me," Dr. Victor apologized and cracked his knuckles. "It is kind of you to help. Frank loves his flowers so."

Dr. Victor picked up a flowerpot and examined the large blossom. As he looked around the greenhouse, the petunia slipped through his fingers and smashed to the floor. Dr. Victor kicked several other plants out of the way as he ran to the destroyed side of the greenhouse. "No, Frank," Dr. Victor cried. "Please tell me you didn't."

He picked up a broken bottle with a large red label. The label read FORMULA BIG. He held the bottle upside down. One green liquid drop oozed out.

"Frank, why did you bring my formula in here?" Dr. Victor's voice was shaky. "Fourteen years of work, ruined. Ruined!" He put his face in his hands and slipped to the floor, sobbing.

Mrs. Jeepers quietly ushered the third-graders out of the greenhouse. "I think Dr. Victor needs some privacy," she said softly.

Liza took one last look at the greenhouse as she went into the museum. Broken pots, glass, and stray flowers

FORMULA
BIG

still covered the floor. As the last drops of rain fell, sunlight shone on Frank cradling Dr. Victor in his arms. Frank groaned as Dr. Victor sobbed. "Ruined, Frank. My hopes for you ruined."

12
Good-bye — For Now!

Mrs. Jeepers and the kids walked down the wet museum steps toward the school bus. The sun peeked through clouds as Frank appeared in the open museum door, his arms full of huge red petunias. He clomped down the steps toward the kids. "Hrrmm."

"I think he wants us to have the plants," Liza said as she took a pot from Frank. Each of her friends took one, too.

"These flowers are beautiful," Melody said.

"They're the prettiest ones I've ever seen," Howie agreed. "And the largest."

"That formula must really work," Eddie mumbled.

"Thank you, Frank," Liza said softly. "For the flowers — and for saving my life."

Frank blushed and looked down at the ground as the kids climbed onto the bus.

"You never did prove Frank wasn't a monster," Liza told Eddie as they drove away.

"Frank can't be a monster," Melody said.

"Why not?" Howie asked.

"Because Bailey City already has a monster." Melody giggled.

"It does?" Eddie asked.

"Yeah," Melody told her friends. "And his name is Eddie!"